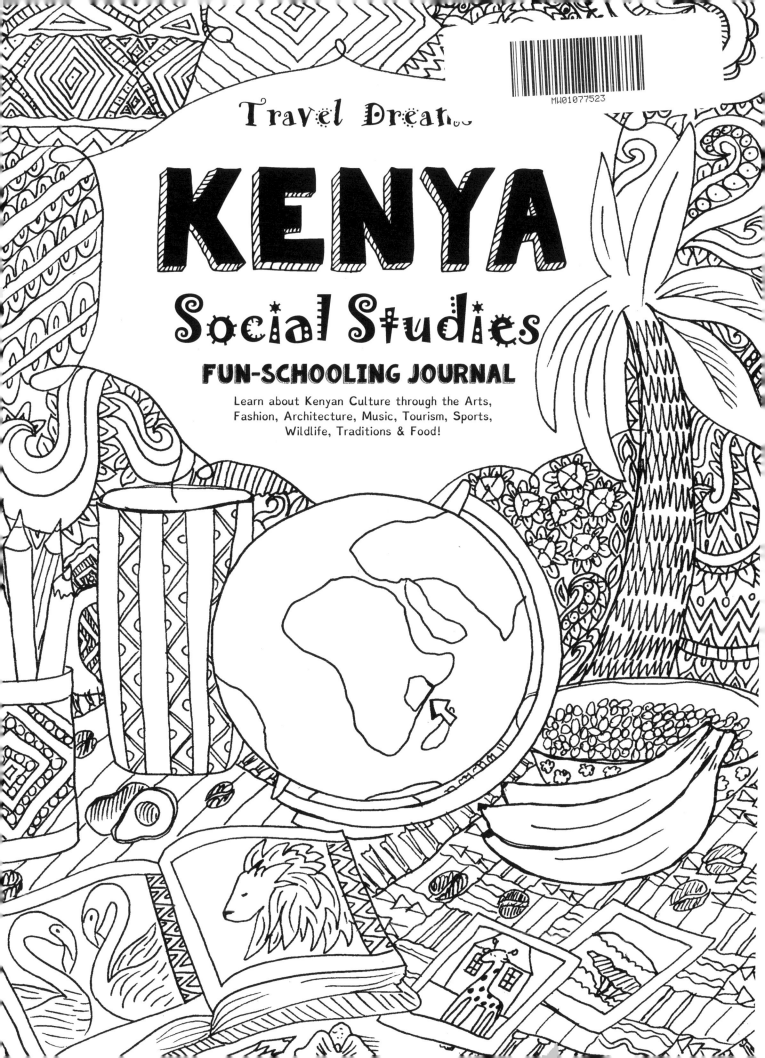

Travel Dreams

KENYA

Social Studies

FUN-SCHOOLING JOURNAL

Learn about Kenyan Culture through the Arts,
Fashion, Architecture, Music, Tourism, Sports,
Wildlife, Traditions & Food!

To hear traditional music from this country listen to

Travel Dreams Geography

AROUND THE WORLD IN 14 SONGS

Search for Amazon Product Number: B072C2QXJS

Around the world in 14 songs is a delightful musical tour of the world. Adults and children will enjoy these original instrumental songs that reflect the authentic style of music that originated on all six major continents. Travel to the rhythm and melody of traditional instruments, and enjoy the fun-filled tunes.

The musical journey begins in Ireland, sweeps across Europe, dances through Asia, Africa and then soars over the ocean to Australia and the Caribbean! After an exciting night at a Smoky Mountain bluegrass festival you will enjoy a siesta in Mexico and finally land in Brazil where you will join the festa in Rio-De-Janeiro.

Music has never been more fun... or educational!

Travel Dreams
KENYA
FUN-SCHOOLING
JOURNAL

An Adventurous Approach
Social Studies

Learn about Kenyan Culture Through the Arts,
Fashion, Architecture, Music, Tourism, Sports,
Wildlife, Traditions & Food!

Travel Dreams
KENYA
Fun-Schooling
Journal

NAME:

Date:

Contact Information:

About Me:

Let's Learn!

Topics & Activities You Can Explore With This Curriculum:

- Ethnic Cooking
- Travel
- History of Interesting Places
- How People Live
- Tourism
- Transportation
- Wildlife and Natural Wonders
- Cultural Traditions
- Natural Disasters

- Famous and Interesting People
- Missionary Stories
- Scientific Discoveries
- Fashion
- Architecture
- Plants
- Animals
- Maps
- Language

KENYA

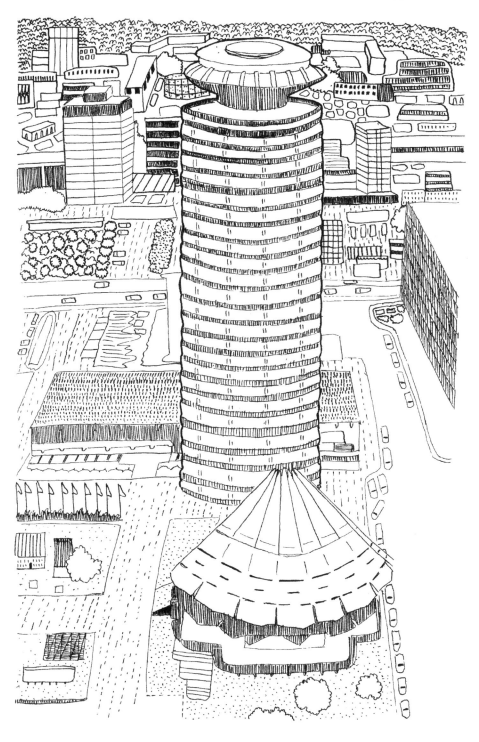

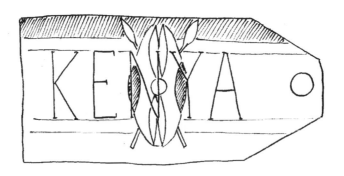

Travel Dreams Fun-School Journal
You are going to learn about Kenya

Teacher & Parent To-Do List:

- Plan a trip to Kenya or just plan a trip to the library or local bookstore.
- Download Google Earth so your child can zoom in and learn more!
- Choose online videos about Kenya so your child can learn about culture, food, tourism, traditions and history.
- Be prepared to help your child choose an ethnic recipe and shop for the ingredients.

Go to the Library or Bookstore to Pick Out:

- Books about Kenya
- One Atlas or Book of Maps
- One Colorful Cookbook with Recipes from Kenya

DRAW THE COVER OF YOUR BOOKS!

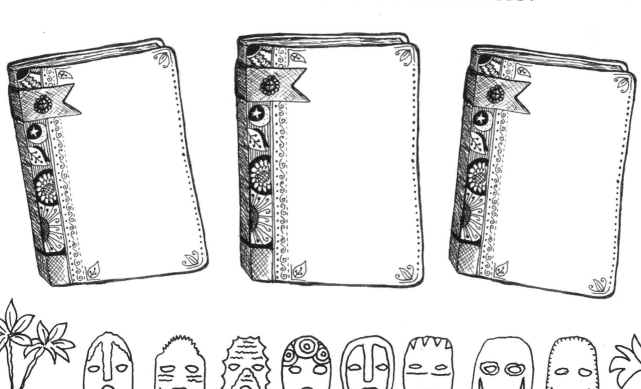

COLOR IN KENYA ON THE MAP

Zoom into Kenya using Google Earth and explore the wonders
of this amazing country!

LABEL THE MAP

Add 15 Interesting Things to this Map!

Write or Draw
Use your Library Books

Popular Foods:	Traditional Clothing:
Draw the Flag:	A Quote or Proverb:
A Historic Event:	A Famous Landmark:

LEARNING TIME

READ A BOOK AND WATCH A VIDEO ABOUT FOOD IN KENYA:

BOOK TITLE:_____

_____

VIDEO TITLE: _____

_____

_____

What did you Learn?

_____

_____

_____

_____

_____

_____

KENYAN CUISINE

What do Kenyan people love to eat?

Can you list **5** of the most popular Kenyan dishes?

1.＿＿＿＿＿＿＿＿＿＿＿＿＿＿＿

2.＿＿＿＿＿＿＿＿＿＿＿＿＿＿＿

3.＿＿＿＿＿＿＿＿＿＿＿＿＿＿＿

4.＿＿＿＿＿＿＿＿＿＿＿＿＿＿＿

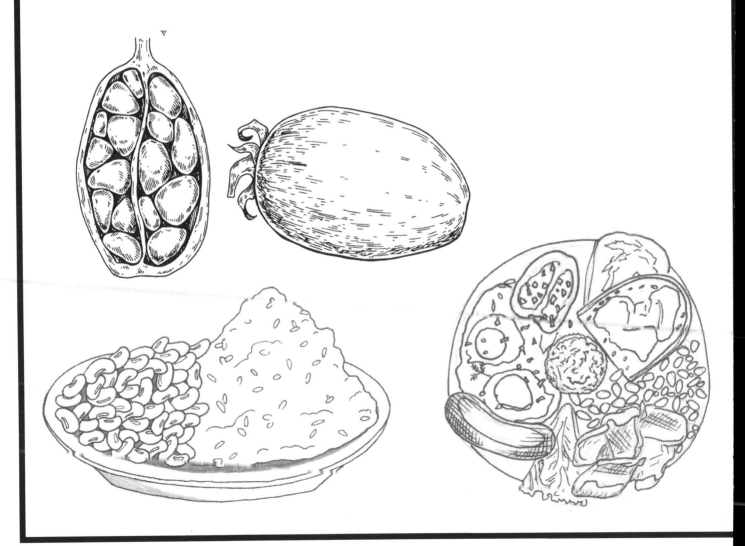

Draw your favorite Kenyan food

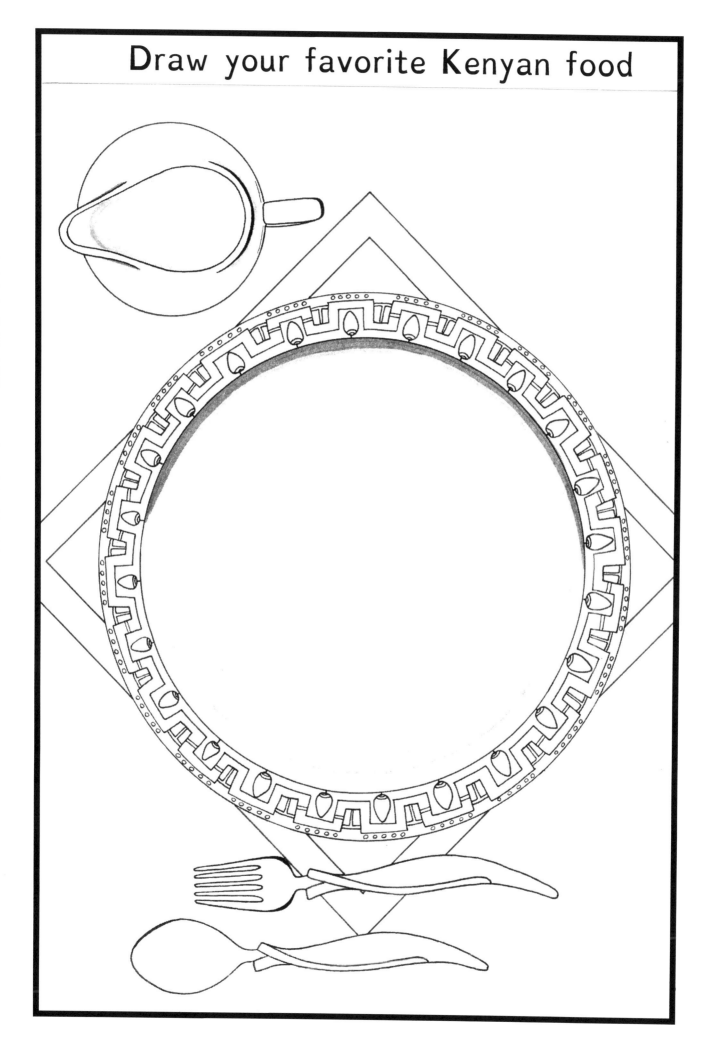

Find a Recipe From
KENYA
TITLE:

_____

Ingredients:

_____ _____

_____ _____

_____ _____

_____ _____

_____ _____

Instructions:

_____

_____

_____

_____

_____

_____

_____

_____

_____

Step by Step Food Prep:

1	2
3	4
5	6

DRAW
THE FOOD
THAT YOU
PREPARED!

RATE THE
RESULTS!
1, 2, 3, 4, 5

Color the words
that best describe
your food:

DELICIOUS
YUMMY
TASTY
GREAT
DELIGHTFUL
OKAY
BLAH!
GROSS
YUCKY
DISGUSTING
STINKY
ICKY

What to Do in Kenya

Create a **COMIC STRIP** showing your dream adventure!

LEARNING TIME

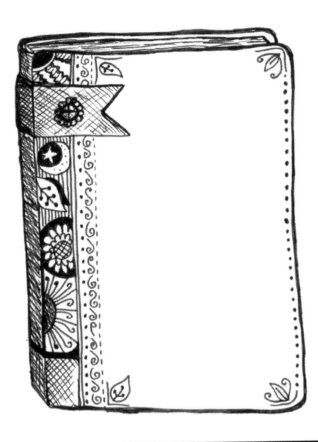

READ A BOOK AND WATCH A VIDEO ABOUT A FAMOUS PERSON

BOOK TITLE:_____

_____

VIDEO TITLE: _____

_____

_____

Write 3 Interesting Biography Facts

_____

_____

_____

_____

_____

_____

All About Style

KENYA

Fashion in the City

_____

_____

_____

MODERN STYLES

Draw yourself dressed like a stylish Kenyan person :

Color The Traditional Costume:

Trace and color this
traditional Female Kenyan costume

Trace and color this traditional Male Kenyan costume

KENYAN HISTORY

Write about a Historic Event

LEARNING TIME

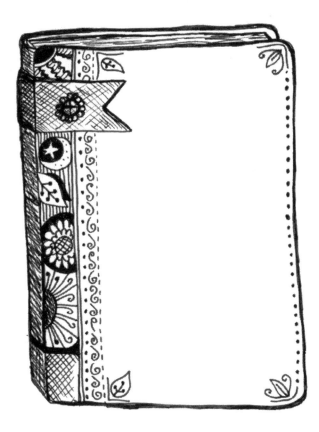

READ A BOOK AND WATCH A VIDEO ABOUT NATURE & WILDLIFE

BOOK TITLE:_____
_____
VIDEO TITLE: _____
_____
_____

Notes:
_____
_____
_____
_____
_____
_____

WHAT ANiMaLS LiVe iN KeNYa?
Can you LiST teN?

1._____
2._____
3._____
4._____
5._____
6._____
7._____
8._____
9._____
10._____

Draw each of the animals

PLANTS IN KENYA

Can you list ten flowers or trees found in Kenya?

1._____

2._____

3._____

4._____

5._____

6._____

7._____

8._____

9._____

10._____

Draw each of the plants

HISTORY OF MUSIC IN KENYA

Write about a famous Kenyan musician:

_____

_____
_____
_____
_____
_____
_____

What instrument did he/she play?

_____

Can you draw it?

A NATIONAL INSTRUMENT

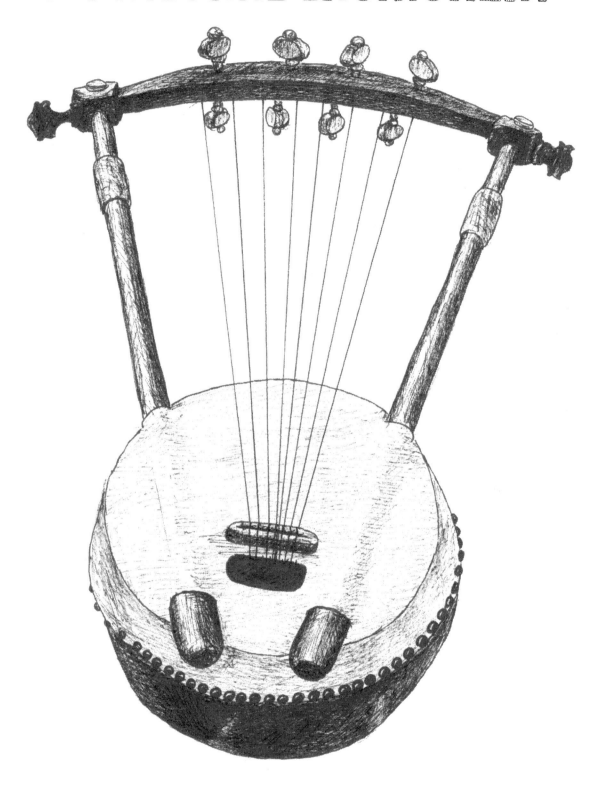

To hear traditional music from this country listen to
Travel Dreams Geography—Around the World in 14 Songs

Track Number & Song Name:
07-Kenya – Climbing Kilimanjaro

KENYAN ART & ENTERTAINMENT

Read a book or watch a documentary about art and entertainment in Kenya

Write down 5 interesting things you learned:

1. _____

2. _____

3. _____

4. _____

5. _____

Draw or doodle in Kenyan style

Write down a quote or a Lyric from a Famous Kenyan poem or song

_____

_____

_____

_____

_____

_____

_____

_____

_____

_____

_____

_____

_____

HISTORY OF TRANSPORTATION IN KENYA

Find 3 interesting facts about Kenyan transportation

1._____
_____
_____

2._____
_____
_____

3._____
_____
_____

Use your imagination and add something to this picture.

Write a short story about this picture

_____

_____

_____

_____

_____

_____

_____

_____

KENYAN INVENTIONS

Read a book or watch a documentary about your favorite Kenyan inventor:

_____

Write down 5 interesting things about his/her life:

1._____
_____

2._____
_____

3._____
_____

4._____
_____

5._____
_____

Write down 3 Kenyan inventions that changed the world:

1. _____

2. _____

3. _____

Draw your Favorite Kenyan invention

KENYAN SPORTS

Read a book or watch a documentary about a popular sport in Kenya:

_____

Write down 5 interesting things about this sport

1. _____

_____

2. _____

_____

3. _____

_____

4. _____

_____

5. _____

_____

DraW a popular KeNyan Sport

KENYAN HOMES
Write about a Family tradition in Kenya

_____

_____

_____

_____

KENYAN TRADITIONS
Draw some traditional Kenyan décor elements

Trace & Color
A TRADITIONAL KENYAN HOME

Design Your Own
KENYAN HOME

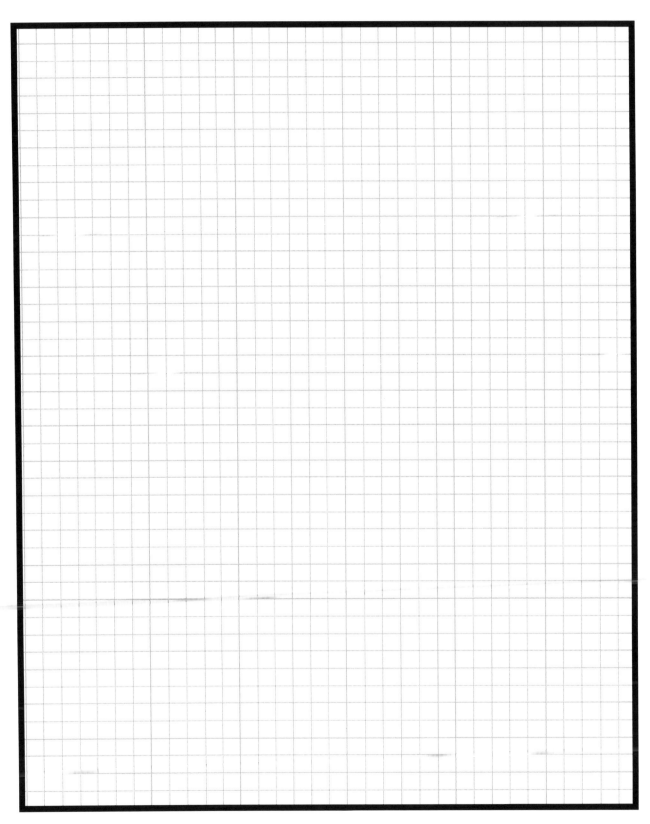

Find and color in the Hidden objects

LEARNING TIME

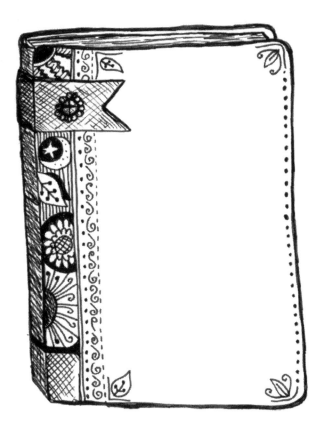

READ A BOOK AND WATCH A VIDEO ABOUT TOURISM & TRAVEL

BOOK TITLE:_____
_____
VIDEO TITLE: _____
_____
_____

Notes:
_____
_____
_____
_____
_____
_____

PLAN A TRIP TO THE CAPITAL OF KENYA

_ _ _ _ _ _ _

Who are you going with?

_____

What are you taking with you?

_____

How long is your trip?

_____

What do you want to see or visit?

_____

PLAN YOUR TRIP
What to Do in
Nairobi

Five Things to Know
when Traveling to
KENYA

1 _____

2 _____

3 _____

4 _____

5 _____

What to Say

Create a **COMIC STRIP** using six Kenyan phrases:

CREATIVE WRITING

Write a story about an imaginary trip to Kenya

Illustrate your Story

Do it Yourself
HOMESCHOOL
JOURNALS
BY THE THINKING TREE, LLC

Made in the USA
Middletown, DE
03 July 2024

56802390R00038